PUFFIN BOOKS

THERE'S A TROLL
AT THE TOP OF OUR TIP

Ann Jungman was born and educated in London; her parents were refugees from Germany. Originally, Ann studied law and intended to be a lawyer, but during a stint of supply teaching, Ann decided she preferred teaching to law and children to lawyers, so she shifted careers. While teaching, Ann got very immersed in children's literature and decided to try her hand at writing. Nearly ninety books later, she's glad she did.

Ann Jungman lives in London, but has spent many years in Australia, and still visits there regularly.

Some other books by Ann Jungman

THERE'S A TROLL AT THE
BOTTOM OF MY GARDEN
THERE'S A TROLL AT THE
BOTTOM OF OUR STREET

SEPTIMOUSE, BIG CHEESE!
SEPTIMOUSE, SUPERMOUSE!

Ann Jungman
There's a Troll at the Top of Our Tip

Illustrated by Doffy Weir

PUFFIN BOOKS

PUFFIN BOOKS

Published by the Penguin Group
Penguin Books Ltd, 27 Wrights Lane, London W8 5TZ, England
Penguin Putnam Inc., 375 Hudson Street, New York, New York 10014, USA
Penguin Books Australia Ltd, Ringwood, Victoria, Australia
Penguin Books Canada Ltd, 10 Alcorn Avenue, Toronto, Ontario, Canada M4V 3B2
Penguin Books (NZ) Ltd, 182–190 Wairau Road, Auckland 10, New Zealand

Penguin Books Ltd, Registered Offices: Harmondsworth, Middlesex, England

First published 1998
1 3 5 7 9 10 8 6 4 2

Text copyright © Ann Jungman, 1998
Illustrations copyright © Doffy Weir, 1998
All rights reserved

The moral right of the author and illustrator has been asserted

Typeset in Times New Roman Schoolbook

Made and printed in England by Clays Ltd, St Ives plc

British Library Cataloguing in Publication Data
A CIP catalogue record for this book is available from the British Library

ISBN 0–140–38835–4

Contents

The Letter

The children of Sebastopol
Avenue were busy playing a
computer game.

"I'm sick of this," said
Patrick.

"So am I," moaned Selima.

"What's wrong with this game?" demanded Darren. "It's good."

"No it isn't!" chorused Selima and Patrick. "It's boring."

Darren laughed. "Well, don't let the troll hear you say that, he goes bonkers when we say we're bored."

"I wish our troll was here," sighed Selima. "It's never boring when he's around, we always have great adventures with our troll."

"I know," complained Patrick. "But he's too busy sorting out the rubbish up at

the tip these days
to have any time for us."

"It was great when we first
found him in the garden
shed, wasn't it?" said Selima.

"Yeah," agreed Darren. "And we had to try and keep him a secret."

"Last summer was even better," chipped in Patrick. "When we all went walking by the canal and the troll fell in."

"Yeah!" cried Selima. "And we even ended up being interviewed on the telly."

Just then there was a loud
knock at the front door. The
children fell over each other to

answer it but Mrs Brook got
there first.

"It's a letter for the troll,"
she told them. "Registered
mail. I had to sign for it."

"Who could be
writing to our troll?"
demanded Selima.

"Maybe it's from the TV programme he was on last year," suggested Mrs Brook. "Or maybe it's from the hospital the troll was in."

"My bet is it's from another troll," joked Darren, and they all laughed.

Patrick studied the letter.
"It looks very official," he
commented. "Maybe
it's important."

"Yes," agreed Darren,
"and I think we should
take it to the troll at work."

"But it's pouring down with rain," protested his mother.

"We'll wrap up," promised Darren. "Please, Mum, we're all bored witless."

"Well, all right," said his mother reluctantly. "But zip up your anoraks, keep your hoods on and don't splash in puddles."

*

So the three friends set off for
the municipal tip, making
good and sure that they
didn't miss a single puddle as
they went. As they got near
to the tip they heard the
familiar sound of the troll
singing.

"Oh I'm a troll, fol-de-rol,
I'm a troll, fol-de-rol,
I'm a troll, fol-de-rol,
And I sort rubbish for a
living,
And I love it, fol-de-rol,
And I wouldn't be doing
anything else,
No, not for five million
pounds, fol-de-rol."

"Hello, troll," the children
all shouted together, to attract
his attention.

"Hello!" yelled the troll,
smiling broadly. "What are

13

you lot doing out in this
weather?"

"We've got a letter for
you," yelled Darren at the
top of his voice. "It may be
important, it came by
registered mail."

"What did you say?" the
troll shouted back.

"A letter – for you," they
all yelled together, and
Darren waved it in the air.

"All right, I'm coming
down," the troll told them.

"But only for a minute, mind. I'm very busy. There seems to be more rubbish than ever and it all has to be sorted."

And he began to walk down the slope of the pile of rubbish.

"Now what's all this fuss about a letter, then?"

"We thought it might be important," Darren explained.

"Hmm," mumbled the troll, opening the letter.

"Well, it's from someone called 'Collect, Clean and Sort'. Never heard of them. I wonder why they want to write to me?"

"Read it," suggested Selima. "Then we'll all find out."

"All right," agreed the troll. "Just hold the umbrella over me so the letter doesn't get wet. Right, here goes."

The Bad News

The troll read the letter and a tear ran down his face.

"What does it say?" asked Darren.

"Please tell us," begged

Selima. "Maybe we can help."

The Troll shook his head and let the letter drop to the ground. Patrick picked it up and read:

COLLECT, CLEAN & SORT

Dear Mr Troll

As you may already know, the firm of Collect, Clean and Sort have taken over collection and distribution of rubbish in your area.

The firm has a very strong policy on employment and we do not feel that a troll, however

committed, is a suitable
employee. In view of your
long and caring service, we
will pay your wages for a
further four weeks.

Please accept our thanks
for all that you have
done to keep the borough
clean.

Yours faithfully

J. S. Sort.

(Managing Director)

"That's crazy," exclaimed
Darren. "Everyone knows
this area was a mess till you
took over."

"We'll all complain,"

agreed Selima. "We'll organize a march and we'll get everyone to write letters."

"Yes," added Patrick. "It's so unfair, everyone will be on your side, troll."

"It's all right," sniffed the troll. "Don't bother yourselves on my behalf.

I'll just go home now, if you don't mind."

And he trudged off, his shoulders slumped over and tears running down his face.

That night when Darren went to get the troll for supper there was a new notice on the door of the troll's hut. It read:

DISTURB THIS TROLL ANY TIME. THIS TROLL IS UNEMPLOYED AND USELESS AND HAS NOTHING TO DO.

"Oh dear," thought Darren. "This doesn't sound good."

"Troll," he called. "Come and have supper. We bought you some special coconut and chocolate chip ice cream and Mum has just made the

best, the most absolutely yummy fudge sauce."

"Tell her thanks," mumbled the troll, "but I'm not hungry. If I'm not working I don't build up an appetite."

When Darren told his parents the news, his mother

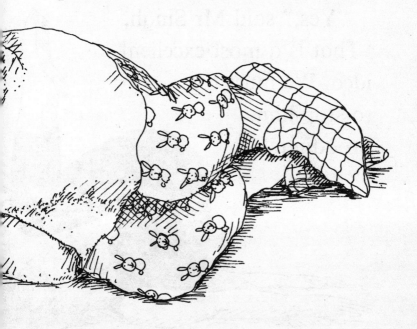

said, "Let's call a meeting and get the Singhs and the Gormans to come."

"What we need to do," declared Mrs Gorman, "is keep the troll busy, keep his mind off what has happened until we can sort things out."

"Yes," said Mr Singh. "That is a most excellent idea. We must try to stop him brooding."

So they drew up a list of
activities for the troll.

On the first day Mrs Singh
took the troll to her yoga
class. The troll joined in but
looked miserable
all the time.

On the second day Mr
Singh had the troll out early,
delivering papers for him.

"It's all right," the troll
told him over a cup of tea.
"But it's kids' work really.
I'm too old for that kind of
thing. I'm used to running
my own show."

Mr Gorman had a word
with the people who ran
Troll's Lock.

"Could you employ the
troll to sit under your bridge
and sing his troll song?" he
asked. "Our troll is so
miserable."

So the troll sat under the
bridge and sang away:

"I'm a troll, fol-de-rol,
I'm a troll, fol-de-rol,
I'm a troll, fol-de-rol,
And I'll eat you for my
supper."

But the weather was very
bad and the children of the
neighbourhood didn't come
to the lock to be scared.

Darren and Selima and Patrick ran backwards and forwards but the troll wandered off, shaking his head and saying, "You're only doing this to please me and you aren't a bit scared, it's a waste of time. I want a proper job. I want my old job back."

The Petition

As the days went by the troll got more and more miserable. He stopped eating altogether and sat around moping.

"Feel like a game of football?" asked Patrick hopefully.

The troll shook his head. "I, the great chess grand master, challenge you to a chess match," declared Darren.

"No way," mumbled the troll.

"Mum says I've got to paint my bedroom," said Selima valiantly, "but I'm really terrible at painting. Would you help?"

"No," said the troll. "I'd only mess it up. I'm no use at anything."

"Something has got to be done," decided Darren. "I can't stand seeing our troll so miserable, and the grown-ups don't know what to do."

"So it's up to us," agreed Selima. "And I've got an idea."

The other two looked at her.

"You know when they were going to build a road through here and everyone signed a paper to stop it? Well, let's get everyone to sign

in support of our troll."

"A petition," yelled
Darren. "That's what it's
called."

"Yes," agreed Patrick.
"You have to make columns
on a piece of paper, for name,
address, and signature."

"And we need a clipboard
to attach it to."

"They've got those at
school, maybe one of the
teachers would lend us one."

So the next day the three
stayed behind after school and
asked their teacher for a
clipboard for their petition.

"A petition?" said Mrs
Khan. "What an excellent
idea. I want to be the first
person to sign and I think you
should tell the school about it

in assembly. That poor sweet troll has been very shabbily treated."

In the morning the three children plucked up all their courage and told the whole school about the troll being unemployed and becoming very sad. After assembly the whole school lined up to sign the petition.

"Look at that," said
Darren proudly. "Only one
day and we've already got
ten pages of signatures."
After school the children

went up and down the streets asking for signatures and no one said "No".

At the weekend they set up a stall down at Troll's Lock and everyone lined up to sign.

"It's a crying shame," they exclaimed. "That troll has done nothing but good. This

area was a real dump before he came, filthy dirty and with that smelly canal running through it. He has made a real difference and I reckon he's had a rotten deal."

Within a week the children

43

had a whole huge box full of tightly packed signatures. Mr Brook drove the children to the head offices of 'Collect, Clean and Sort', and the four of them staggered in, buckling under the weight of the box.

"What's that you've got there?" asked the doorman.

"It's a petition," Mr Brook told him. "We've got thousands, no, maybe tens of thousands, of signatures protesting at the sacking of our troll."

"Oh yeah, I heard about that," sniffed the doorman.

"Got a space for me to sign?" And he wrote his name in the very last space.

"Would you deliver it to Mr Sort himself?" asked Patrick anxiously. "It's very, very, important."

"You have my word," the doorman assured him. "But the boss never changes his mind, I'm afraid, so don't hold your breath."

Darren's Idea

After the failure of the petition the troll got even more miserable. He just sat in his hut and wouldn't talk to anyone.

The three families were

holding another council of
war, when suddenly Patrick's
father said, "I've had enough!
I've been unemployed at
least three times, and no one
got a petition together for
me or arranged little jobs for
me here and there or held

councils of war about me. I
mean, it's time the troll
helped himself a little bit,
and I'm going down to his
shed to tell him so right
now."

And Mr Gorman strode
down the garden path and

disappeared into the darkness. Mrs Brook opened the french windows so that they could hear what was being said.

"Troll," they heard, "I've come to tell you that I think you're behaving like a wimp and unless you start to help yourself, I for one am not going to support you any longer. I mean, those children have been walking the streets getting signatures for that petition and everyone else is bending over backwards to help, but you just sit here and feel sorry for yourself. Now,

you're not the first one to be made unemployed and you won't be the last, so are you going to sulk or are you going to fight?"

There was a long silence.

"Oh dear," sighed Mrs Gorman. "Paddy has such a hot temper and he always speaks his mind. I hope the troll can take it."

"He's so easily upset," agreed Selima.

"Dad's right," interrupted

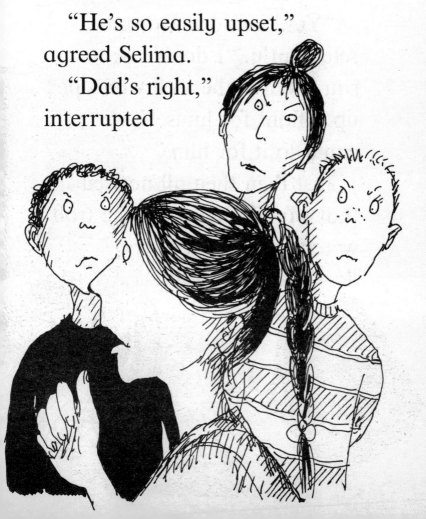

Patrick. "The troll did just accept things and walk away."

"That is the truth, Patrick," said Mr Singh.

"Yes," nodded Darren reluctantly. "I don't like to say it but if the troll won't put up a fight for himself, we can't do it for him."

Just then they all noticed that Mr Gorman and the troll were walking out of the darkness. The troll came indoors,

sat on a chair and looked at
his feet.

"I owe you all an apology,"

he said in a small voice. "I've
been very silly. As of this
evening I am going to fill my
time up till I think of a way
to get my job back."

"Hurray!" shouted the
three families.

"Would a touch of ice cream help?" asked Mrs Brook.

"It certainly would," said the troll. "Now don't you move, you have done a full day's work. I am going to fetch it. How many for ice cream?"

So they all sat round eating ice cream and feeling much relieved that the troll was his old self again.

"I'm beginning to get an idea," said Darren, smiling mysteriously. "When it's ready I'll tell you all about it.

"Darren," groaned Patrick and Selima. "Don't be a tease. Go on, tell us."

"Not yet," insisted Darren. "But soon."

After that the troll
cleaned up
the houses

and did the
shopping

and went to visit
people in hospital

and played
with the children
too young
to go to school

THE THREE
BILLY GOATS
GRUFF

and weeded the gardens and
went to yoga once a week
and started to learn Spanish.

One evening he even cooked
supper for everyone.

"That was a fantastic
curry, troll," declared Mrs
Singh. "Well done."

Everyone muttered
agreement, and the troll
grinned with delight as he
packed the dishes into the
dishwasher.

"Well, the house has

certainly looked good since the troll took over the running of it," declared Mrs Brook. "He's much tidier than me."

"Yes," agreed Mr Brook. "The street's loss is our gain."

"The street's looking awful," nodded Mr Singh. "Almost as bad as it was before the troll came along."

"Yes, if you ask me
Mr Collect, Mr Clean and
Mr Sort don't know what
they're doing," declared
Mrs Gorman. "Not employ
trolls, indeed. I never heard
such nonsense."

"All we have to do is
convince them of that," stated
Darren.

"You look to me, son, like
you've got one of your ideas,"
said Mr Brook nervously.
"And that usually means

trouble, so I'm saying to you in advance, in front of everyone, forget it."

"No idea, Dad," said Darren, smiling innocently. But no one believed him.

Sorted!

The next day Selima and Patrick met Darren on the way to school.

"What's the idea, then, Darren?" they asked.

"This," replied Darren, as

he kicked a black plastic bag
of rubbish into the road.

"You mean make a terrible
mess?" asked Selima.

Darren nodded, scattering
newspaper into the gardens
as he walked past.

"You can't do that," cried
Patrick. "It's disgusting, and
we'll get into no end of
trouble!"

"Do you want our troll to
get his job back or not?"
demanded Darren.

"Of course I do, but there
must be a better way."

"If you can think of one," shouted Darren, "I'll do it."

"Darren's right," declared Selima. "So let's enjoy being litterbugs."

So the three children had fun making as much mess as they could. They went up one street and down another leaving a smelly trail of litter behind them.

"We're going to be very late for school," said Selima nervously.

"Do you want to help our troll or not?" demanded Darren.

"Of course I want to help, but my mum will go nuts if

she hears I
bunked off
school."

"Mine too,"
mumbled Patrick.

"Then you two go on to
school and I'll save the troll
on my own," snapped
Darren.

At that
moment
he felt a
heavy hand
on his shoulder.

"So what are you up to,
sonny?" came a stern voice.

There stood a tall
policeman with a cross
expression on his face.

"We're not just being
naughty," Selima told him.
"We're doing this to help
someone."

"Oh yes," said the policeman. "And who would that be, then?"

"Our troll," Darren told him.

"Your troll! What, the one who got the sack?"

"Yes," said the children. "He's our friend and we want to show Collect, Clean and Sort that he's really needed."

"I see," said the policeman, and he looked a bit less cross.

"Well, I'm quite

sympathetic. I saw that troll
on the television and he
seemed decent enough."

"Oh, he is," the children
assured him.

"Still, you had no business
doing this in the street. Come
on, I'm taking you all home

and I'm going to have a word
with your parents."

Only Mr Brook was home
when the children arrived
with the policeman.
When he heard
what had

happened he
was so angry he
sent them all upstairs
while he decided what
to do with them.

The troll made the
policeman a cup of tea.

"It's all my fault," he
moaned. "I got the children
into trouble. What can I do to
help them?"

"You've got loyal friends there," commented the policeman. "I remember thinking that when I saw you on television."

"Television!" yelled the troll. "That's the answer!" And he undid his apron and

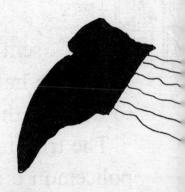

ran out of the house, shouting, "Tell them I'm going to talk to my friends at the television!"

The troll took a cab to the TV headquarters and raced up the stairs and into the interview studio.

"Hello, troll," cried the interviewer, kissing him on both cheeks. "And how are you?"

"I got the sack," wept the troll, and then he told her the whole story.

"That's shocking," she said angrily. "Leave it with me, troll, I'll sort it out. It's a good story, you just watch my programme tomorrow night."

The next night they all
huddled round the TV.
"There she is!" yelled
the troll.

"Good evening, everyone," said the interviewer. "Now here is a clip of an interview I did with a wonderful troll last year."

And the interview was shown.

"Now this poor troll has been deprived of his job just because he's a troll," continued the interviewer indignantly. "He kept his area tidier than anyone can remember, but look at it now." Some scenes of the streets the children had dirtied came on to the screen.

"So I would like you to ring in on 0073562 and let me know if you think the troll should get his job back. And at the end of the programme I'll tell you the result."

The troll bit his nails till the end of the programme.

"We've got the result of our troll poll, 782 for, 3 against, and what's more we've had Mr Sort on the line offering the troll his job back. I hope you're watching, troll!" smiled the interviewer, and she blew kisses at him.

That night they all had a big celebration

and the next morning the troll
got up early to go to work.
He climbed to the top of the
tip and put up a notice:

THERE'S A TROLL AT THE
TOP OF THIS TIP AND IT'S
THANKS TO MY FRIENDS
AND ALL THE LOCAL
PEOPLE.
I LOVE YOU ALL.

TROLL XXX